Rabbits Eat Lettuce Without Any Dressing *and Other Rhyming Stories*

by Marian H. Miller

To order RABBITS EAT LETTUCE WITHOUT ANY DRESSING
and OTHER RHYMING STORIES:
Book Order Department...... 1-800-788-7654 .....or
bookorders@rosedogbooks.com ....or
Yahoo! Store at www.rosedogbookstore.com

RoseDog ❖ Books
PITTSBURGH, PENNSYLVANIA 15238

RoseDog Books
585 Alpha Drive
Suite 103
Pittsburgh, PA 15238
Visit our website at *www.rosedogbookstore.com*

ISBN: 978-1-4809-6620-8
eISBN: 978-1-4809-6597-3

This book is in loving memory of my mother, Tina Heiden,
who instilled in me a love for writing poetry and
for the many hours she spent reading to me when I was a child.

Acknowledgment

With special appreciation and thanks to my daughter, Lynn Robin Miller, my sisters, Eleanor Graber and Phyllis Richards, and to my friends, Miriam Schuman, Gladys Levinson and Ann Caflun, who patiently listened to me reciting my poems and for their continued support and encouragement.

Rabbits Eat Lettuce Without any Dressing

I just thought of something that's really distressing
Rabbits eat lettuce without any dressing
Bears eat honey without muffins or toast
Foxes eat chicken that they don't even roast
Monkeys in trees eat bananas they peel
With no corn flakes or milk to round out their meal

A squirrel eats nuts till he fills up his belly
Without ever tasting peanut butter and jelly
Sea gulls and pelicans dive for fish
With scales and bones, can
that be a good dish?
Cows eat grass, they can munch it all day
Horses live on a diet of hay
A lion brings animals to eat in his lair
Frogs eat flies that they catch in mid air

Chickens eat corn without any salt
And birds eat worms, but it isn't their fault
Humans are lucky with so varied a diet
So when Mom cooks something different,
I think I will try it!!

Dreaming of Horses

I once had a ride on a pony
He was pulling a little red cart
He wore a straw hat with a flower
And I loved him right from the start

His owner allowed me to feed him
He gave me a few yellow grains
Then we walked him around in a circle
And I held on to the reins

Ever since then I love ponies
And I love horses too
To be with them, I've made a plan
I will tell you what I'll do

I'll get a job as a groomer
In a stable in back of the track
I'll brush a horse till he shines so bright
You can see your face in his back

I'll give him cool water to drink
And enough oats for him to eat
Sometimes I'll let him have sugar
Because horses love something sweet

I will get a big broom
And I'll sweep the floor
When it looks like it's clean
I'll sweep it some more

I will do such a good job
That the owner will say
"If you want to ride my horse
You may ride him today"

Then I'll put on his bit and his saddle
And I'll sit on him straight and tall
My feet will be in the stirrups
And I'll do my best not to fall

I will ride that horse over hill and dale
I will let him drink from a stream
I will be the best horseman ever
That, you see, is my dream!

Best Friends

Cookie and I were best friends
As close as best friends can be
She told me all of her secrets
And I told her all about me

We played together every day
We would ride our bikes or run
No matter what we found to do
We always would have fun

At night we spoke on the telephone
And Mom would always say
"Whatever can you talk about?"
You just saw her all day

We hardly ever had a fight
That's why it is so unfair
As soon as Cindy came around
It was as though I wasn't there

I really do feel terrible
Sometimes I want to shout
It's just not right that I should be
The girl who is left out

My mom says I'm too sensitive
And shouldn't feel this way
That there really is no reason why
The three of us can't play

But it seems they do not want me
And they did not tell my why
Did I change? What could be wrong?
It makes me want to cry

My dad told me to cheer up
He said "Put on a smile"
He said I'll find someone new
In a little while

My parents explained to me
That sometimes things must end
But I want things back – the way they were
When Cookie was my friend

Boating

My grandpa has a boat
That he sails upon the sea
He promised that if I am good
Some day he will take me

If I close my eyes
I can pretend I'm on that boat
The water swirling round about
And keeping us afloat

The sun sparkles on the water
Like my mother's diamond ring
The birds are flying all around
So close you hear them sing

And when I take a deep breath
The air is crisp and clear
I've heard about pollution
But there isn't any here

The sky above is brilliant blue
The clouds a cotton white
Nature seems a part of me
The smells, the sounds, the sight

Grandpa is the captain
And I'm his new first mate
Grandpa knows where we can fish
And I'm in charge of bait

I help to turn the steering wheel
And keep a watchful eye
For lobster pots and other boats
That may be passing by

I'll ride the waves
I'll catch a fish
I'll sail the seas
If I get my wish

A Christmas Surprise

There was frost outside on Christmas Eve
The streets were white with snow
Our house was warm and cozy
The fireplace was aglow

Our tree sparkled at the window
We had lights strung everywhere
And it would be very soon
That Santa would be here

I knew I should be happy
And I shouldn't fret
But the gift I wanted most
Was one I wouldn't get

I wanted a pet to hold in my arms
Some cute little furry thing
A cat or a dog that would be my own
But that's not what Santa would bring

Animals need a lot of care
My parents work all day
And I'm too young to care for a pet
While they are both away

Suddenly our doorbell rang
But no person could be seen
There was only a cardboard box
Tied in ribbons of red and green

Inside the box was a kitten
Shivering from the cold
I picked her up and held her close
She was so good to hold

She snuggled up against me
And I could hear her purr
As I gently kissed her head
And stroked her silky fur

Mom and Dad had no idea
How a kitten came our way
But as long as she was here
They said that she could stay

They said that I was old enough
To care for this wonderful pet
And that is how this became
My very best Christmas yet!

A Scary Night

Evil hung like clouds
In a starless night
The air I breathed
Was thick with fright

The streets were dark
No moon could be seen
A cold wind blew
T'was Halloween

The presence of ghosts
Could be felt everywhere
I knew I could touch them
If I would dare

The silence was eery
But for an occasional woosh
A black cat was hiding
Behind every bush

Suddenly I heard laughter
The sound was weird
Could it be witches?
I was so scared

Where could I hide?
I crawled under the bed
But the noise I was hearing
Still pounded my head

Giggles and chatter
That's what I heard
I could make out voices
But not a word

I went to the door
My heart skipped a beat
The children outside
Sang out "Trick or Treat!"

Cook's Little Helper

My mother really loves to cook
She is known as a gourmet
She says the things that you enjoy
Are never work, they're play

My mom collects her recipes
In a big thick book
I never know from day to day
What she'll decide to cook

Mom says the meals she plans
Depend on what she buys
That is why the food we eat
Always comes as a surprise

I go with Mom to the market
Where we buy vegetables and meat
She says that green and yellow veggies
Are the healthiest to eat

We buy fruit that is in season
And cereal and beans
We buy milk, eggs and butter
And all sorts of salad greens

I like to help my mother
I help her quite a lot
I like to help her plan the meals
And look inside the pot

I also like to roll the dough
When Mom decides to bake
I am the special taster
Of her pies and cake

Some day when I am bigger
I know what I will do
I'll cook and bake like Mother
And be a gourmet too!

Do I Have to Eat This?

The food upon my plate was blue
I hardly knew what I should do
It surely didn't look like meat
But Mother said that I must eat

Blue is the color of summer skies
And also the color of my best friend's eyes
And when I fell over Daddy' shoe
The bump I had was black and blue

But blue food!
I wasn't in the mood
Should I try it?
Or create a riot

Mom said I must taste the food on my plate
Before I decide it's something I hate
Why did I squirm?
It wasn't a worm

It was only blue food
I must not be rude
I must not be hasty
It might even be tasty

Maybe I'll try it as long as I'm able
And then if I'm lucky I'll run from the table
Where would I go?
I didn't know

What could it be?
I looked closer to see
I just couldn't tell
It didn't even smell

I finally decided that I would be strong
But what if it turned out that I was wrong?
Was this a trick?
Would I get sick?

My mother loved me
That I knew
Even if her food was blue
I decided to brave it
But I just didn't crave it

What a taste!
Is this a dream?
It seems to me that it's ice cream
That's what it is
I kid you not
Blueberry ice cream and I like it a lot!!

Dreams

Sometimes when I am fast asleep
I see a picture show
My parents say I've had a dream
And they seem to know

They say that dreams must happen
Dreams are something they can't fix
That it is my imagination
Playing little tricks

My dreams are all in color
In every shade and hue
It is hard for me to understand
That they aren't true

The things I see seem very real
Though they're not real at all
Sometimes I dream I'm tiny
And other times I'm tall

When I dreamed about a church
I thought I heard the bell
When I was running with a ball
I really thought I fell

I've dreamed of people that I love
And dreamed of strangers too
I've dreamed of being happy
And I've dreamed of being blue

I have seen before my eyes
An angel with white wings
I saw a fairy princess
And the handsomest of kings

But when I have a scary dream
I find myself in tears
And then I call to Mom or Dad
To chase away my fears

Far Away Places

In Switzerland the Alps stand tall,
Majestic and proud
Reaching higher than the eye can see
Their snowcaps in a cloud

Venice is a city
Where everything's afloat
If you want to get from here to there
You have to take a boat

The bright skies of Madrid
Make night seem like day
The wide streets have sections
Where children can play

Have I been to those places?
Switzerland, Italy and Spain
The answer is "no"
And I will explain

I have been there through books
Because I can read
And can follow the path
Where books alone lead

Books are the keys
That can open the door
To a far away world
That we can explore

We can see in our minds
How places can look
Once we learn how to read
Our first simple book

Flu Blues

This morning when I woke up
I did not feel so good
My nose just kept on running
My throat was made of wood

My head seemed very heavy
Just like a bowling ball
I felt a little dizzy
And was worried that I'd fall

My mother called the doctor
He told her what to do
He said that I must stay in bed
I probably had the flu

Mom went out to buy a chicken
To make home made chicken soup
She said that it's a natural cure
For colds and cramps and croup

Grandma called up on the phone
To make sure that I'm all right
She said that this flu germ
Is something I must fight

I must drink lots of water
And I must get lots of rest
That's the part of being sick
I really like the best

My pillows propped about me
I feel like royalty
Since I can't go to anyone
They all must come to me

Dad brings me books and games
So that I won't be bored
I really think that being sick
Is more fun than being cured!

I Really Miss My Grandma

I really miss my grandma
She lives so far away
The telephone's not quite enough
There is so much to say

My father said that in the summer
If everyone is well
We'll take a trip to visit her
And sleep in a motel

At my grandmother's house
There is so much to see
Albums of photographs
And even some of me

Where Grandma lives most folks are old
You hardly see a child
Except for Christmas time and summers
And then the place goes wild

Grandchildren running everywhere
And jumping in the pool
Splashing, laughing, having fun
And trying to keep cool

Grandmothers are in their kitchens
Preparing food to eat
Baking pies and cookies
And every kind of treat

Dreaming up things for us to do
In case the weather is bad
Making sure that every holiday
Is the best we've ever had

I cannot wait till summer's here
I'm counting every day
I really miss my grandma
She lives so far away

If I Could Go to Africa

If I could go to Africa
Where animals roam free
I would see a tall giraffe
Having dinner from a tree

To reach the highest branches
He wouldn't have to try
His graceful neck would be so long
His head would touch the sky

Perhaps I'd see a lion
And even hear its roar
It would frighten all the animals
And scare me even more

Elephants would stroll about
Their trunks swaying to and fro
Great big ones and babies
All walking in a row

If I could go to Africa
Monkeys I would see
Hanging by tails to branches
Swinging from tree to tree

Monkeys come in many sizes
In many colors too
And they make the best of parents
Just like me and you

I'd see rhinos, deer and zebras
A hippopotamus or more
I might even see a snake
One cannot tell for sure

But until I get to Africa
There's not much I can do
But look at pictures in a book
And see animals in the zoo!

Lucky

I have a dog named Lucky
And lucky he must be
I found him wandering all alone
And brought him home with me

The day I first saw Lucky
He was hungry and so thin
He was looking for some food
Around a garbage bin

My mom and I bought dog food
And gave him some to eat
He drank a bowl of water
For him it was a treat

Lucky was really filthy
Full of dirt and grime
You could tell he had not been bathed
For a long long time

He also didn't smell so good
I had to hold my nose
But he just wagged his tail
As we rinsed him with a hose

My dad said Lucky strayed from home
And we must find his master
The police would be able to help us
And they could find him faster

The police tried and we tried to find him
But Lucky still stayed lost
I wanted Lucky to be my dog
I had my fingers crossed

Finally Dad said I could keep him
His master could not be found
If I had not saved Lucky
He would have been sent to the pound

So I was able to keep him
And he is a wonderful pet
And he is happy because he was lucky
But I am luckier yet!

My Great Grandma

I have a great grandmother
Who is really very old
She wears a shawl around her neck
Because she's always cold

She cannot walk too well these days
And has to use a cane
But though she can't get around too much
I never hear her complain

Her home is filled with pictures
Of Mom and Dad and me
Cousins, aunts and uncles
And folks I seldom see

She knows Aunt Sara had the flu
And Mary caught a cold
And Cindy's daughter's boyfriend
Gave her a ring of gold

She knows Uncle Eric's baby cries
And keeps him up all night
And Mrs. Johnson's dog and cat
Just had another fight

She knows it snowed again in Michigan
And there's a heat wave in L.A.
She'll tell you the score of the football game
And how they'll do today

She keeps up with all her TV shows
And can tell you all the news
And whether you want to know or not
She'll tell you all her views

She knows I got an A in reading
And what I learn in school
Great Grandma may seem old and frail
But boy, I think she's cool!

Rainy Day Fun

When I look out my window
I see a rainy day
I guess there's not much I can do
But stay inside and play

Perhaps I'll watch a video
Or cartoons on TV
I have played so many computer games
They're not much fun for me

In my room I have toy soldiers
They're packed up in a box
An electric train, some pretty dolls
And even wooden blocks

If I took that box
And put it on the floor
It could be a fortress
For the soldiers to explore

I could dress up all my dolls
And pretend they're queens and kings
I could turn them into puppets
Just by adding strings

I could take my blocks
And make a building tall
I can take one out
And watch the building fall

I could make a track
On which to ride my train
Oh I'm so glad
The weatherman said rain!

Thanksgiving

The turkey was naked
It seemed such a shame
No feathers at all
Did he have to his name

He was shiny and white
And really quite fat
He would be dinner for us
With some for the cat

Such good smells filled the house
I can hardly explain
How it made my mouth water
And my tummy complain

Thanksgiving is fun
And always a treat
With so much to do
And so much to eat

Turkey with stuffing
Dressing and yams
Oysters and walnuts
Cranberries and ham

Corn and potatoes
Puddings and rice
Pumpkin pie, ice cream
And everything nice

When I sat down for dinner
As I was taught
I said thank you to God
For all that he brought

The Animal Shelter

In our town we have a shelter
Where animals come to stay
Each one was brought there because
That animal was a stray

A stray is very lonely
It does not have a home
It might be lost or just "put out"
And simply has to roam

The people who work at the shelter
Are really very kind
No matter how scruffy an animal is
They do not seem to mind

The puppies and kittens get a bath
They also get some food
Soon even the saddest one of all
Is in a better mood

I went to visit the shelter
To see what I would find
I saw cats in all colors and sizes
And dogs of every kind

I saw mama cats licking their kittens
And puppies all scampering about
I saw sad eyed dogs in cages
"Take me" they all seemed to shout

Suddenly something happened
The very best thing yet
My dad whispered in my ear
"Why don't you pick out a pet?"

The Argument

My daddy is a saver
My mom throws things out
Mom gave away Dad's red shirt
And he began to shout

Mom said that Dad didn't wear that shirt
For well over a year
And now some poor fellow
Will have a shirt to wear

I do not like when my parents fight
It gives me quite a scare
I put my fingers in my ears
So I cannot hear

My parents said that even grownups
Do not always agree
Like when my friend wants to play outdoors
And I'd rather watch TV

And even though they disagree
They still love one another
And will always be to me
A loving dad and mother

They said that an argument
Is really not a fight
And it doesn't even matter
Who is wrong or right

But that every single person
Should have the right to say
Exactly what is on his mind
In a respectful way

My parents then made up and laughed
And both said that they thought
The red shirt was not as important
As the lesson that it taught

The New Baby

A baby is coming to our house
My mom and dad said so
I asked if it was a girl or boy
They said they didn't know

My parents really want it
I can't imagine why
They said it can't do anything
But eat and sleep and cry

I cannot help but wonder
What it will be like
Will I have to share my toys?
Will it ride my bike?

Does it mean that I won't be
The one my folks adore?
Does it mean that I won't be
So special anymore?

My parents said, "don't worry"
And special I will be
Because no one in this whole wide world
Can be the same as me

The love they have goes round and round
Like a circle without end
No matter how much is given
There is always more to spend

Babies are so helpless
And very very small
I'm sure that next to this one
I'll seem ten feet tall

My mother says she'll need my help
She'll have so much to do
It makes me feel like I'm grown up
And quite important too

It might be nice when baby comes
I might like it at that
But if babies are so much trouble
Can't we just get a cat?

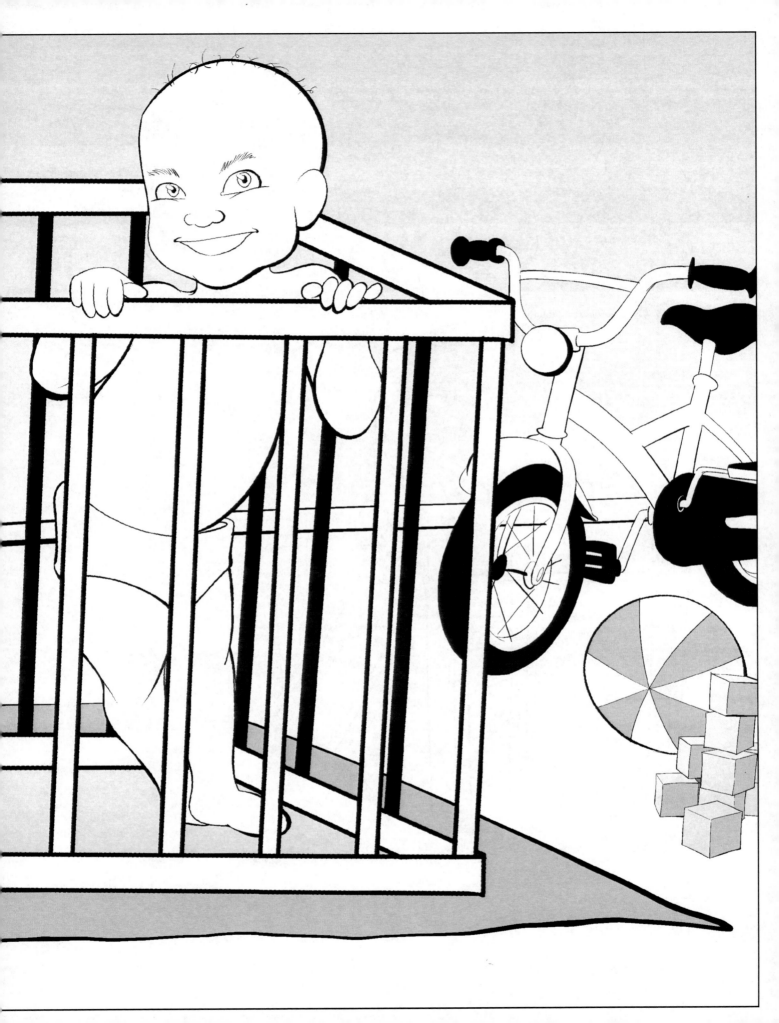

Wait Until You're Older

"Wait until you're older"
That's all that people say
No matter what I want to do
Or what I'd like to play

My brother is great at soccer
He hits a ball with his head
I sure would like to join the team
"When you're older," my brother said

The playground has a ladder
The kids climb from rung to rung
It doesn't seem so hard to do
But Mom says I'm too young

In winter some kids skate on ice
That is something I'd like to try
My dad says it's too dangerous
For one as young as I

I asked if I could stay up late
And do things that grownups do
My parents told me
Just be patient."
"When you're older, you can too

I would like to be an astronaut
And fly up to the moon
I was told I must be older
Right now is much too soon

My uncle works on a big machine
He says it's called a rig
He promised I may go on it
Some day when I am big

Some guys I know swim in a lake
They really have a ball
Can you guess what they said to me?
They said that I'm too small

My parents say for older folks
The time goes much too fast

If I must wait to be their age
I don't think I can last

Summer Day

I woke up one morning
On a lovely summer day
And I thought I'd find some friends
Who would like to come and play

I knocked on their doors
And called them on the phone
But it seems they all were gone
And I'd have to play alone

What could I do on this summer day?
I asked a bird but he hopped away
And then he did what birds do best
He flew into a tree to build a nest

What could I do I asked a cat?
She purred very softly from where she sat
She didn't want to walk or run
Just stretched herself out in the sun

What could I do I asked a bee?
She circled round my head and buzzed at me
Then she went into a dive
And quickly flew back to her hive

What could I do I asked a frog?
He croaked once or twice as he sat on his log
And as I watched he seemed to shrug
Then I saw him eat a bug

What could I do I asked a butterfly?
But she fluttered off in the summer sky
Her wings sparkling with colors bright
It really was a pretty sight

What could I do I asked a rose?
Her sweet perfume tickled my nose
Both delicate and strong she seemed
While on her petals sunlight gleamed

What could I do I asked a tree?
It stood straight and tall and just ignored me
Its head of leaves creating shade
While waiting for the sun to fade

What could I do?
The day had passed before I knew
And I had been for many hours
Among the animals and flowers

What could I do?
What could I do?
I asked myself
but I already knew

I must enjoy the birds and the bees
The pretty flowers, the graceful trees
All God's creatures that come my way
On a lovely summer day

WHY?

Why do the stars come out at night?
Where do they go by day?
When the birdies sing and chirp
What do you think they say?

Why do the trees turn green in spring?
Why do the brooks run dry?
When I run and fly my kite
What makes it go so high?

Why does an elephant have a trunk
When I have a nose?
Why does a duck have webbed feet
When I have ten toes?

Who put the moon up in the sky?
How come it doesn't fall?
It seems to me it should come right down
Like a bouncing ball

Why must Grandpa shave each day
Or else he'll have a beard?
On his head he has no hair
I really think it's weird

There is so much I want to learn
I don't know where to start
I'm really glad that Mom and Dad
Are so very smart

They answer all my questions
At least they seem to try
For how else can I understand
Unless I ask them WHY?